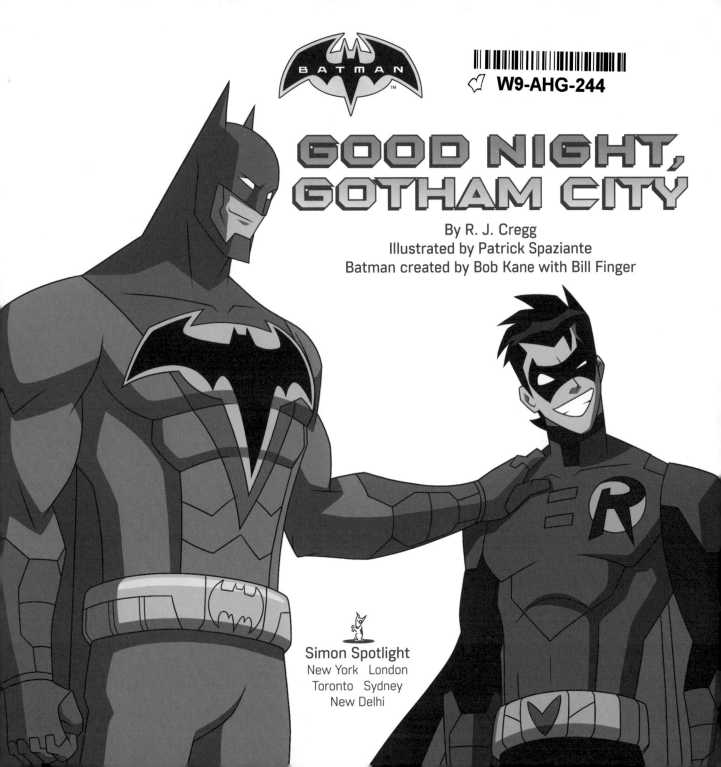

GOOD NIGHT, GOTHAM CITY

By R. J. Cregg
Illustrated by Patrick Spaziante
Batman created by Bob Kane with Bill Finger

Simon Spotlight
New York   London
Toronto   Sydney
New Delhi

SIMON SPOTLIGHT
An imprint of Simon & Schuster Children's Publishing Division
1230 Avenue of the Americas, New York, New York 10020
This Simon Spotlight paperback edition October 2017
All rights reserved, including the right of reproduction in whole or in part in any form.
SIMON SPOTLIGHT and colophon are registered trademarks of Simon & Schuster, Inc.
For information about special discounts for bulk purchases, please contact Simon & Schuster Special Sales
at 1-866-506-1949 or business@simonandschuster.com.
Manufactured in the United States of America 0917 LAK
10 9 8 7 6 5 4 3 2 1
ISBN 978-1-5344-0417-5
ISBN 978-1-5344-0418-2 (eBook)

It's nighttime in Gotham City, and all is well. The Joker is locked up, and the Bat-Signal is off.

"Okay, Robin," Batman says, "it's time to go home."

"Since it's a quiet night, could you give me a driving lesson?" Robin asks.

"And risk a broken Batmobile?" Batman says. "Not tonight."

"Then could I take a spin in the Bat-Mech?" Robin asks.

"And risk broken buildings?"
Batman says. "No."

"Well, how about we fly over Gotham City," Robin says. Then he yawns.
"Just to make sure there's nothing else we should do . . . ."

"Okay, you win," Batman says, engaging the Batwing. "But pay attention. I'll show you how I know we're done for the night."

"I check on Arkham Asylum. I confirm that the guards are on guard and the inmates are sleeping. Double-check on the Joker; sometimes he is faking."

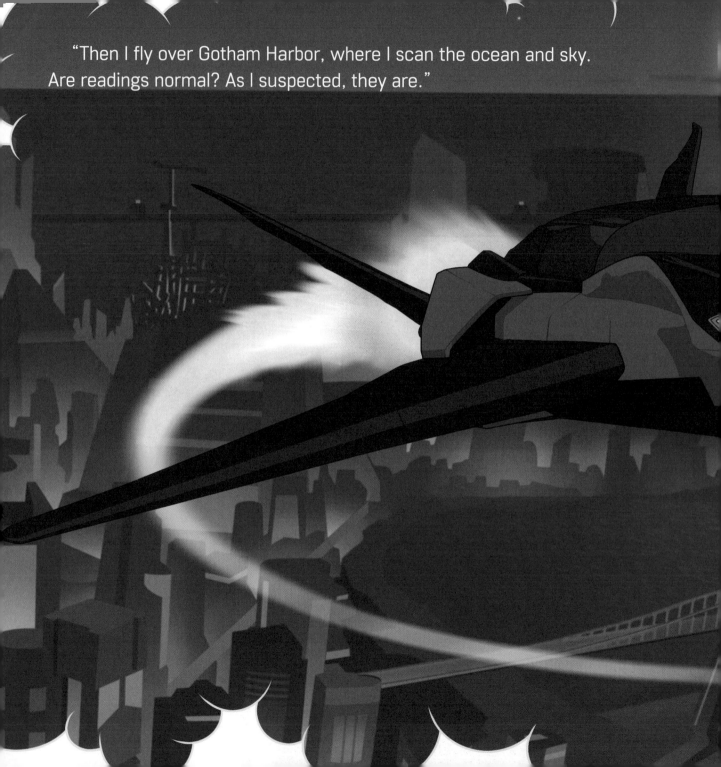

"Then I fly over Gotham Harbor, where I scan the ocean and sky. Are readings normal? As I suspected, they are."

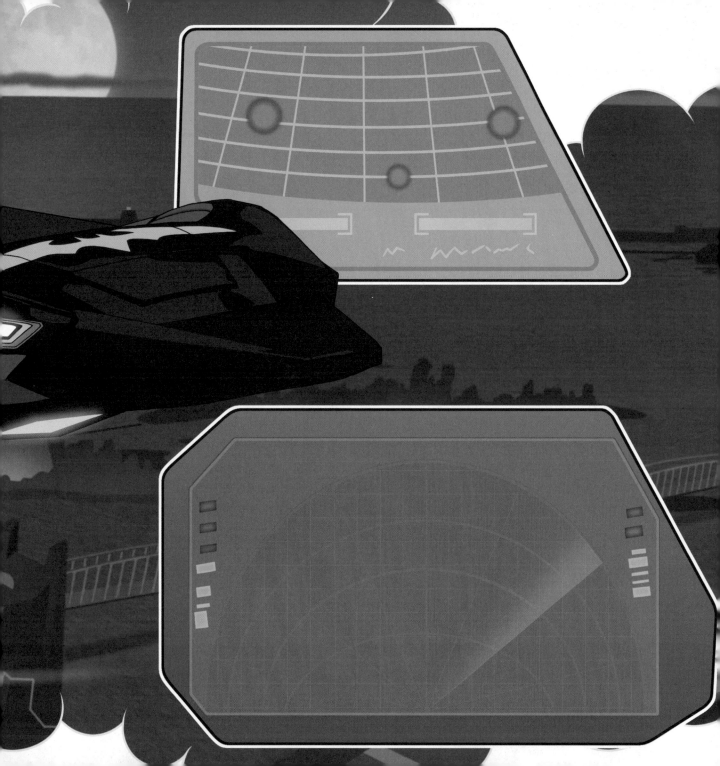

"Lastly, I look at the city from somewhere up high. I see no trouble to stop. There are no battles to win. Thermal readings tell me the citizens are safe in their homes. Our work here is done. Now I should be in bed."

Operating system update available. Please wait.

"Back at the Batcave, there are a few things to do. I park the Batmobile in its place so I know where it is. It's right where I need it when there's no time to waste. I put the Batcomputer in a low-power mode. It saves energy and keeps the system running smooth."

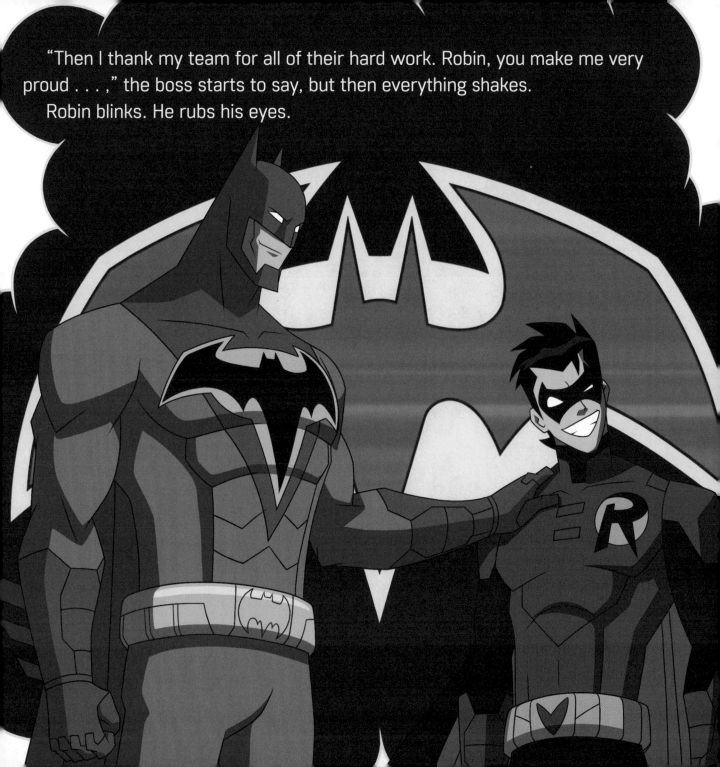

"Then I thank my team for all of their hard work. Robin, you make me very proud . . . ," the boss starts to say, but then everything shakes.
Robin blinks. He rubs his eyes.

"Wake up, Robin," Batman says. "You fell asleep on the way."

"That can't be true," Robin says. "We saw so many things. We saw Arkham and the harbor. We saw the whole city sleeping."

"You must have been dreaming," Batman says. "Now go to bed. I don't think you realize how tired you are."

"You're right, boss," Robin says. "I will say good night . . ."

"Good night, Joker, you villain. Sleep tight in your cell."

"Good night, Commissioner Gordon. Thanks for keeping watch until dawn."

"Good night, Alfred, my friend.
Thanks for locking the door."

"Good night, Robin," Batman says. "Please get some rest."
Robin nods, waves, and climbs up the stairs.

Soon everyone is asleep—even Batman.
Good night, Gotham City.

GO TO SLEEP LIKE A HERO:

To wake up ready to save the day, follow these steps each night.

- ☐ Finish the day's work. Lock up the bad guys and make sure the citizens are safe.

- ☐ Shut down the tech. Put everything in its place. Ready your secret headquarters for tomorrow's action.

- ☐ Change into your sleeping uniform.

- ☐ Wash away the day's adventures. Pay special attention to face and teeth.

- ☐ Choose a book to read. May I suggest a story about super heroes?

- ☐ Climb, swing, or leap into bed.

- ☐ Ask yourself important questions:
  What heroic things did I do today?
  How can I be a better hero tomorrow?
  Is my sidekick's birthday soon?

- ☐ Read your book. Are you getting sleepy yet?

- ☐ Check the sky for signs of trouble.

- ☐ Breathe in. Breathe out. Turn off the light. The citizens will need you again soon.

SLEEP WELL, HERO!

(REPRODUCIBLE)